E BER
Berenstain, Stan
The Berenstain Bears count
their blessings

021313

The Berenstain Bears
COUNT THEIR
BLESSINGS

Small bears get big eyes
when they take off and roam,
and sometimes forget
all the good stuff at home.

A First Time Book®

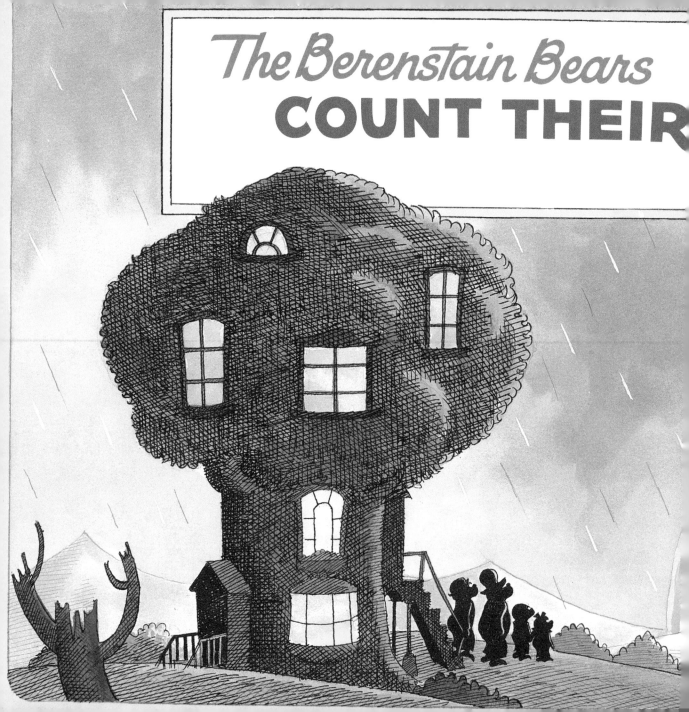

The Berenstain Bears
COUNT THEIR

BLESSINGS

Stan & Jan Berenstain

Random House 🏠 New York

Copyright © 1995 by Berenstain Enterprises, Inc. All rights reserved.
Published in the United States by Random House Children's Books,
a division of Random House, Inc., New York.
Random House and the colophon are registered trademarks of Random House, Inc.
First Time Books and the colophon are registered trademarks of Berenstain Enterprises, Inc.
randomhouse.com/kids   BerenstainBears.com
Library of Congress Cataloging-in-Publication Data
Berenstain, Stan. The Berenstain Bears count their blessings / Stan & Jan Berenstain.
   p. cm. — (First time books)
Summary: During a frightful thunderstorm, Brother and Sister Bear learn that Mama and
Papa's love and protection are better blessings than more Bearbie dolls and video games.
ISBN 978-0-679-87707-3 (pbk.) — ISBN 978-0-307-97878-3 (ebook)
[1. Bears—Fiction. 2. Thunderstorms—Fiction. 3. Family Life—Fiction.]
I. Berenstain, Jan. II. Title. III. Series: Berenstain, Stan. First time books.
PZ7.B4483Bec 1995 [E]—dc20 95-1629
Printed in the United States of America 40 39 38 37 36 35 34 33 32 31 30 29 28 27 26 25

"Mama," said Sister Bear one day after school, "may I go over to Lizzy's house to play this afternoon?"

"Yes, you may," said Mama Bear. "But be sure not to leave a mess for Lizzy's mom, and be sure to be home in time for supper."

As Mama watched Sister skipping happily over the hill to Lizzy's house, she sighed. She knew exactly what was going to happen when Sister got home. And it wasn't just when she got home from Lizzy's. It was the same thing when she got home from Anna's, or Queenie's.

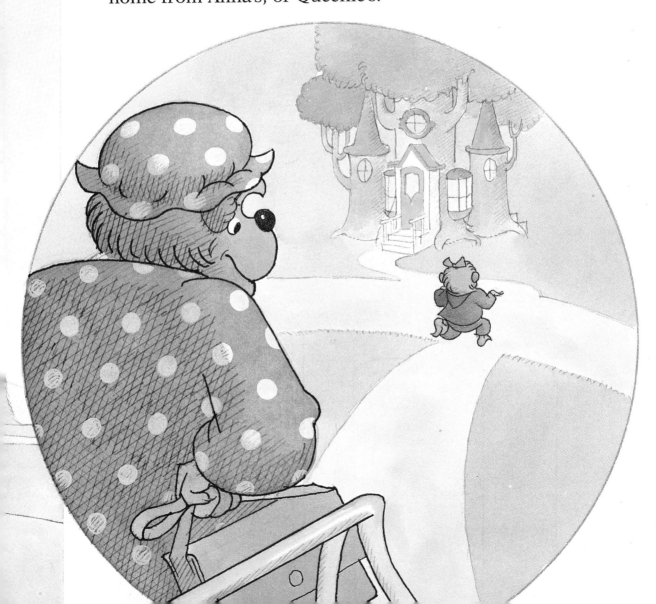

"Anna's got her own phone in her room!" Sister would complain. Or, "Queenie's got her own phone *and* her own TV in her room!" But Lizzy's was the worst. That was because Lizzy had the biggest collection of Bearbie dolls, ever.

"But you have a Bearbie doll," Mama would say. "And your Bearbie has lovely clothes."

"But Lizzy has *lots* of Bearbies!" complained Sister. "She's got High Fashion Bearbie, Supersport Bearbie, Tropical Bearbie, Motorcycle Bearbie, and Just Married Bearbie—and Just Married Bearbie has a whole trousseau!"

Then Mama usually said, "Please, Sister! I've heard quite enough about Lizzy's Bearbie collection!"

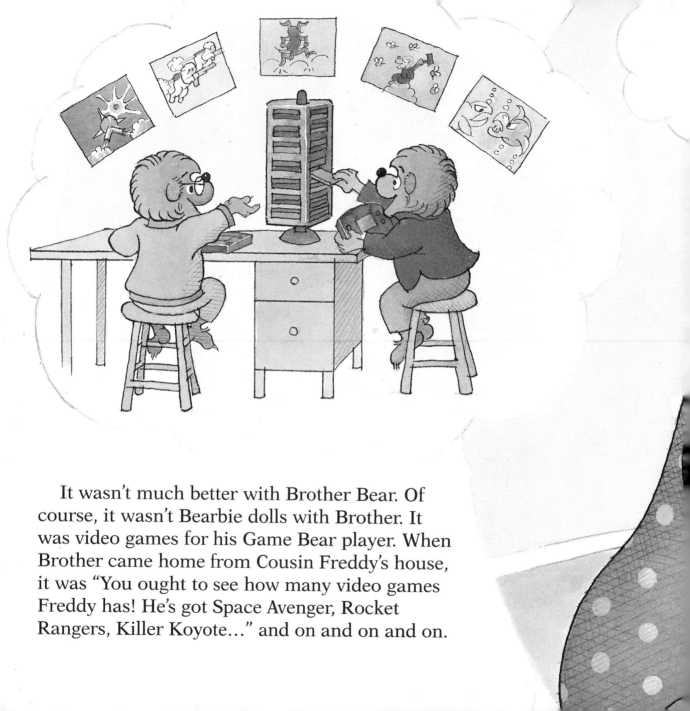

It wasn't much better with Brother Bear. Of course, it wasn't Bearbie dolls with Brother. It was video games for his Game Bear player. When Brother came home from Cousin Freddy's house, it was "You ought to see how many video games Freddy has! He's got Space Avenger, Rocket Rangers, Killer Koyote…" and on and on and on.

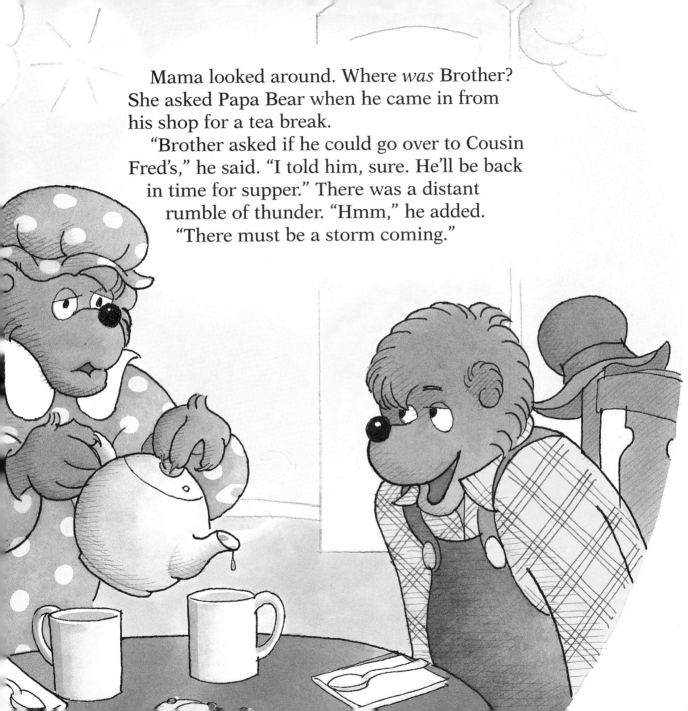

Mama looked around. Where *was* Brother? She asked Papa Bear when he came in from his shop for a tea break.

"Brother asked if he could go over to Cousin Fred's," he said. "I told him, sure. He'll be back in time for supper." There was a distant rumble of thunder. "Hmm," he added. "There must be a storm coming."

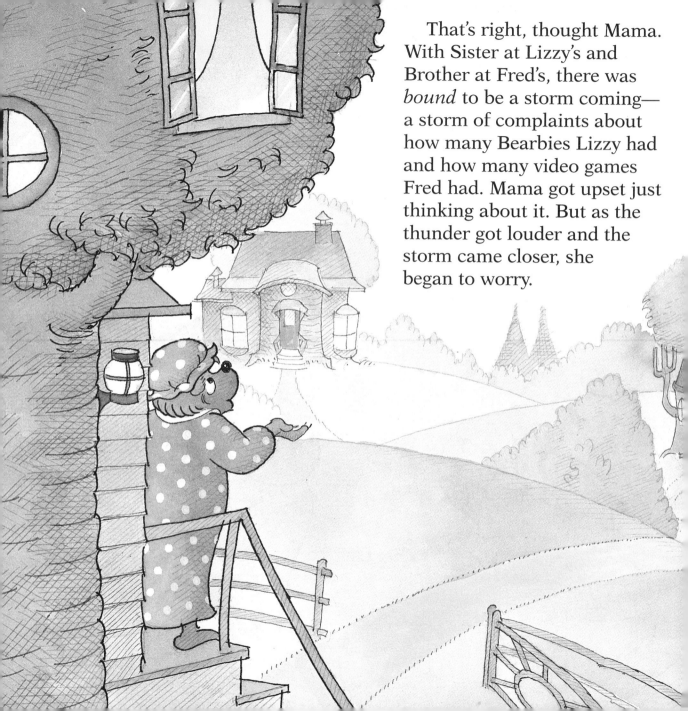

That's right, thought Mama. With Sister at Lizzy's and Brother at Fred's, there was *bound* to be a storm coming— a storm of complaints about how many Bearbies Lizzy had and how many video games Fred had. Mama got upset just thinking about it. But as the thunder got louder and the storm came closer, she began to worry.

She was about to call to have the cubs sent home when she heard them coming up the front steps. They came in the door just ahead of the rain. It didn't take long for the complaining to start.

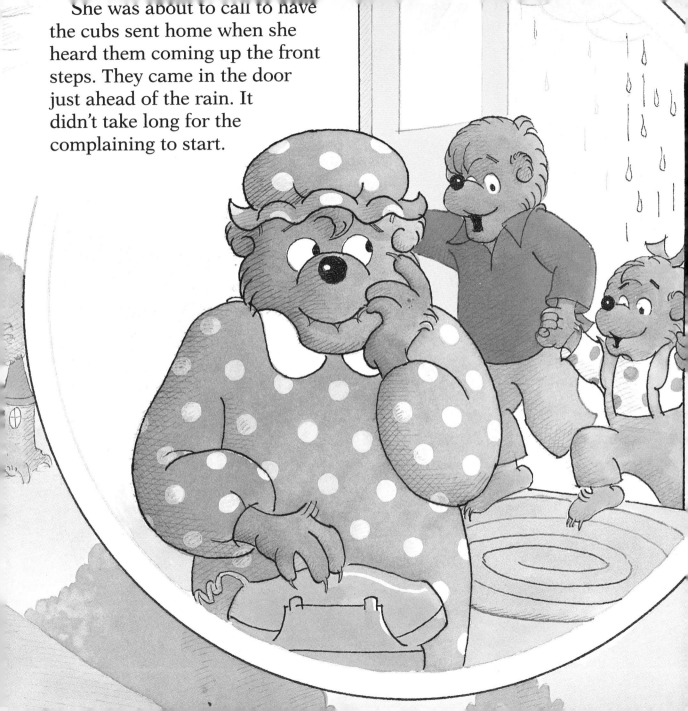

Lizzy just got *Equestrienne* Bearbie!" said Sister. "It's brand-new! It comes with riding clothes and a beautiful horse!"

"You think *that's* something?" cried Brother. "Cousin Fred's got three new video games! Three!"

"Now look, you two!" said Mama. "I've heard quite enough about what you *don't* have. It would be very nice if you would start appreciating the things you *do* have. It's called 'counting your blessings.'"

Just then, there was a big streak of lightning, followed by a big clap of thunder, and the rain started coming down very hard. The cubs weren't exactly afraid of lightning and thunder, but this looked as if it was going to be a really big storm, and they were a little nervous.

"Well," said Mama, "like this warm, cozy house that protects us against the weather. That's one blessing." Now it was really pouring. The wind was whipping the curtains and blowing rain into the house. Mama and Papa rushed about, closing windows.

There was another lightning
flash and another thunderclap.

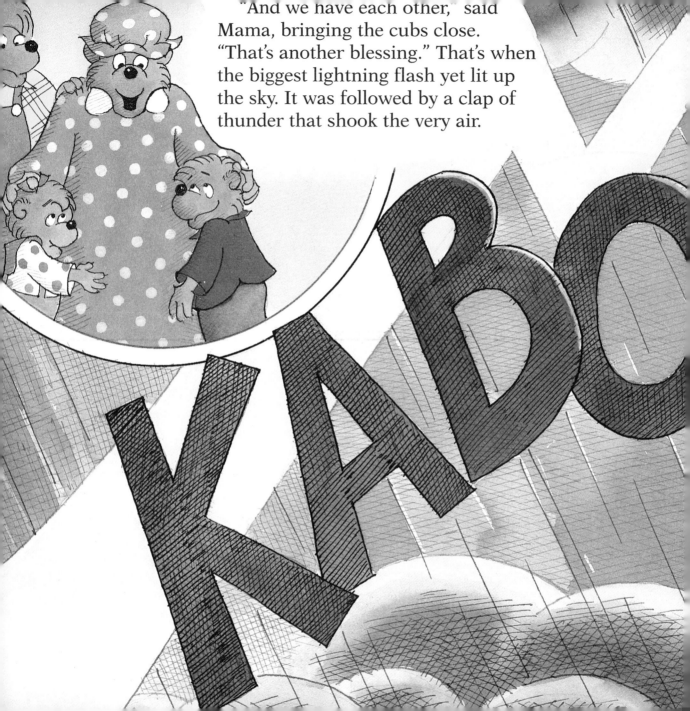

"And we have each other," said Mama, bringing the cubs close. "That's another blessing." That's when the biggest lightning flash yet lit up the sky. It was followed by a clap of thunder that shook the very air.

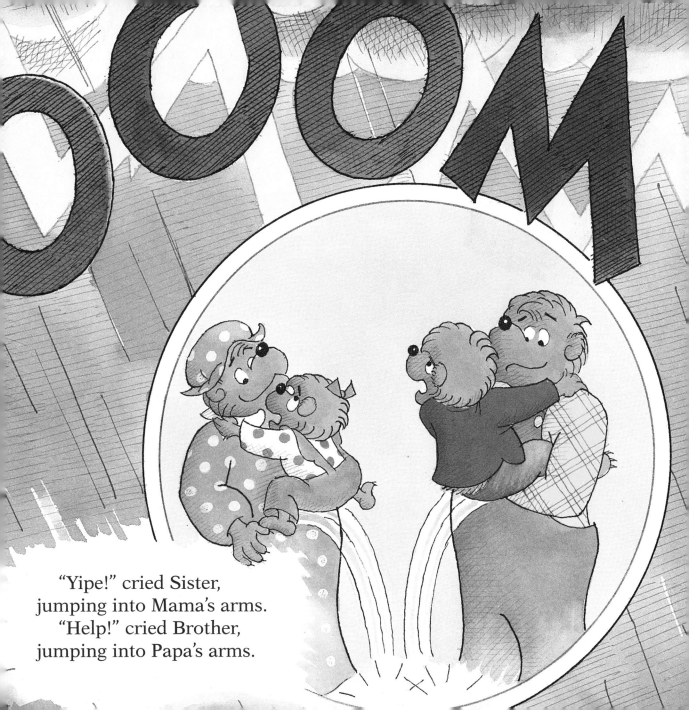

"Yipe!" cried Sister,
jumping into Mama's arms.
"Help!" cried Brother,
jumping into Papa's arms.

"And you've got a mama and papa who love you," said Mama. The lights started to flicker. Then, after a few flickers, they went out.

"And you have a papa who knows how to make a fire in the fireplace," said Papa. Soon he had a cheery fire roaring.

"And a mama who knows how to make cocoa over it," said Mama. She hung a cook pot over the fire. Soon they were sitting in the glow of the fire, sipping hot, sweet cocoa. Mmm! What a blessing that was!

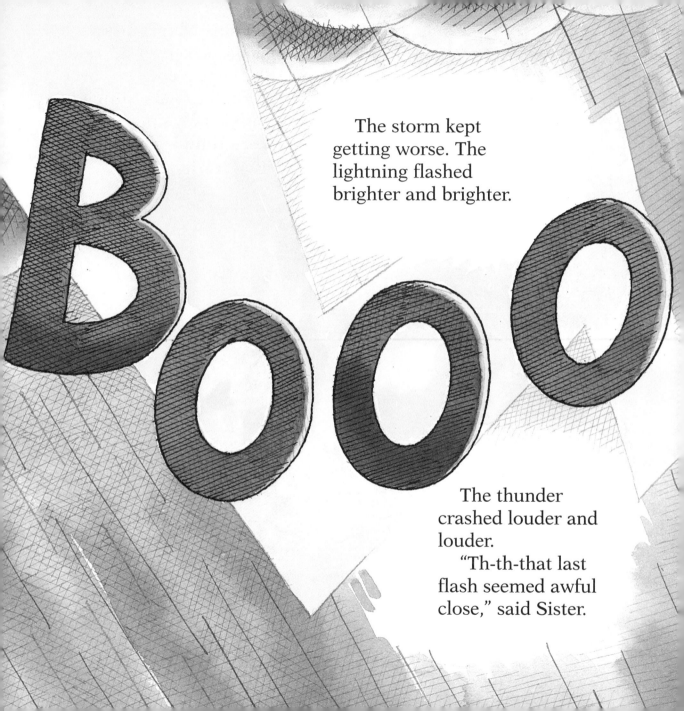

The storm kept getting worse. The lightning flashed brighter and brighter.

The thunder crashed louder and louder.

"Th-th-that last flash seemed awful close," said Sister.

Nothing to worry about," said Papa. "It was at least five thousand feet away."

"How can you tell?" asked Brother.

"Easy," said Papa. "You see, sound travels a lot slower than light. So when you see the flash, start counting the seconds—one…two…three…—until you hear the thunder. Then you figure about a thousand feet for each second." Just then there was a flash.

The cubs started counting.
"One…two…three…" On "four" there was a big thunderclap.
"That flash was about four thousand feet away!" said Sister.
"Very good!" said Papa.

BOOOOMM

Outside, the storm raged on.

But inside their sturdy tree house, the Bear
family was cozy and warm. As the storm grew
worse, they sipped cocoa and counted out the
thunder. The counting helped. Papa explained
what lightning and thunder were. Lightning
was a big electrical flash that traveled
between storm clouds and burned up the air.
Thunder was the sound of air rushing in to
the burnt space. That helped too.

Gradually the storm eased. The rain slowed and stopped, and the lights came back on. The Bear family sighed a big sigh of relief.

Then Sister started counting again.

"Why are you counting, dear?" asked Mama. "The storm is over."

"I'm doing what you said, Mama," she said. "I'm counting my blessings."

So while Papa set the table and Mama started supper, Sister went upstairs to play with her Bearbie doll, and Brother tried to reach the next level on one of his video games.

"You know, my dear," said Papa. "There are birthdays and Christmas coming. Do you have any ideas for the cubs?"

"I thought perhaps a Just Married Bearbie for Sister and a couple of video games for Brother might be nice," Mama said. "What do you think?"

"I think we should count *our* blessings too," said Papa.